When Feelings Get Too BIG

Marion Rhines

When Feelings Get Too Big

This is a work of fiction. All of the characters, names, incidents, organizations, and dialogue in this novel are either the products of the author's imagination or are used fictitiously.

iUniverse books may be ordered through booksellers or by contacting:

iUniverse
1663 Liberty Drive
Bloomington, IN 47403
www.iuniverse.com
844-349-9409

Because of the dynamic nature of the Internet, any web addresses or links contained in this book may have changed since publication and may no longer be valid. The views expressed in this work are solely those of the author and do not necessarily reflect the views of the publisher, and the publisher hereby disclaims any responsibility for them.

ISBN: 978-1-6632-0929-0 (sc)
ISBN: 978-1-6632-0931-3 (hc)
ISBN: 978-1-6632-0930-6 (e)

Library of Congress Control Number: 2020918054

Print information available on the last page.

iUniverse rev. date: 09/23/2020

Foreword

The feelings of rejection, abandonment, and betrayal can be overwhelming for adults who know how to process feelings and how to put them into perspective.

Adults can understand another person's faults, failings, and flaws, and not absorb the guilt, blame, and shame that accompany feeling unwanted and unloved. Children can't.

When those big feelings fill a child's head and heart before they have the words and cognitive ability to describe them, feelings can overtake them. This shows in their behaviors-the only form of communication they have.

They don't know that pain subsides and that better times are ahead. They don't know what comes next. They don't know who to trust. They don't know what is true, because everything they thought was true before is no longer true for them.

When they are in the scariest time of their lives, they can't understand rules and consequences. They can't understand why their world exploded. They don't know what they do not know.

What they do sense is genuine loving kindness. That is the best salve on a wounded little soul.

Rhonda Sciortino
Chairperson, Successful Survivors Foundation

Hi, my name is Jake. I'm eight years old. Sometimes I have a hard time understanding how I feel. But that's okay. I can always ask my parents or another adult for help…and you can, too! Let's look at feelings together.

Feeling overwhelmed is hard on me. It happens when I encounter loud things like automatic hand dryers or toilets that flush by themselves. All I can do is put my hands over my ears and back away. When noises are too loud, I put on my headphones. That really makes a difference. When people are yelling at each other on tv or in a movie, it makes me scared. My stomach feels jumbled up and I want to cry.

Sometimes when I feel angry, I feel like I might explode. I walk around and use my HULK voice and say, "Hulk angry." When I get like that I talk to my sister, Libby. She says, "It will be okay, kid." She calls me "kid." We go outside and sit on the swings. Libby helps me feel better.

When I started kindergarten, I was so afraid of other children. All I could do was lay on the floor and calm myself down. It took me *weeks* before I felt comfortable doing things with my classmates. Then I met Ellie. She could tell when I needed help. And one day, I did it! I played with my friends.

One thing I really get excited about is going on vacation. I really like to stay in a hotel. I make sure and take some movies to watch if it rains. I like the beach, but the pool is my favorite. The sand does not bother you too much in a pool.

I am not sure if it happens to you, but I get stressed out eating food. I do not like for certain foods to touch each other or foods that are mixed like soups, stews, or casseroles. I do love spaghetti and pizza. My parents do not always understand me, and I sometimes get in trouble for being too picky. They need to understand I am doing the best I can to eat what they give me. I do not like feeling this way. My dad does make special things for me when he knows we are having something I struggle with for dinner.

Having sensory issues can be very frustrating. When it comes to my clothes, they must be exactly right. I cannot focus when they are uncomfortable. If any of my clothes have a hole in them, I do not wear them anymore. I also must change if I get wet or dirty. Sometimes sleeping on my bed is weird. I like to sleep in my sleeping bag on top of my covers. Pulling the sleeping bag up around me makes me feel safe.

I have been afraid of animals most of my life. I like dogs, but they scare me when they bark too loud. We have two dogs, Dasher and Dorian. Cats really scare me. When we were looking at our new house to see if we wanted to buy it, I thought the cat that lived there came with the house. Luckily, it moved with its owners. My brothers and I do horse lessons with Mrs. Beth. She is great. I used to be afraid of horses. It has taken me three years, but now I can brush a horse, give them a treat, and drive a buggy.

Feeling disappointed is never fun. We were supposed to visit friends out of town. Unfortunately, there were some travel restrictions that kept us from visiting them. Instead, I had to talk to them on the phone. Hearing their voices on the phone is nice, but nothing beats a big hug in person.

Sometimes I feel lonely. When I feel like this, my mom or dad play with me. I play card games or go to movies with my mom. I play video games with my dad.

I do not know about you, but it is especially important to me to know what the weather will be like every day. I check the weather to know what clothes to wear to school. Do I need a jacket? Should I wear my water boots? Can I wear my tank top, shorts, and sandals? That is my favorite outfit. I would wear this every day if I could. I think it is important to be prepared.

I was born before I was supposed to be, so I was very small. Because of that, I have had to see lots of doctors. Going to the doctor makes me very anxious. I worry about it for days before it happens. I am afraid that I must get shots. The nurse lets me know ahead of time what to expect at the visit. Sometimes I do have to get shots and I cry some. Most of the time it turns out the doctor just looks in my ears, nose, and throat and makes me say AAHHH. I have trouble with my ears and need tubes most of the time. Otherwise, I would stay sick and miss lots of school.

One of the best feelings is when I am at school and I can do all my work. Sometimes I do have trouble with my homework. It usually means I did not understand the instructions. My teacher helps me when I get stuck. I feel proud when I paint a nice picture in art or when I have typed all my spelling words. I feel great when I know I am doing a good job.

We have talked about a lot of feelings. The best one of them all is love. I love my family and friends and I know they love me. We do not always agree on everything, but who does? I am very thankful for them…and for you. Feelings can be big and scary when you experience them. Just know you are not alone. Ask someone for help when you are not sure how to feel. That way your feelings will never get too big.

After the Story

*How could you tell Jake had problems understanding how he feels?

*What did Jake do to get help with the loud noises?

*What did Jake do when he felt angry? Who can you talk to?

*What do you do when you get nervous?

*What things make you excited?

*What do you do when your parents do not understand you?

*Are you afraid of animals?

*What things cause you to feel disappointed?

*What makes you feel lonely?

*Do you like going to the doctor?

*What makes you feel most proud?

*In what ways does your family show you that they love you?

About the Author

Marion Rhines lives in Knoxville, TN, with her husband and five children. She is the Executive Director for the Tennessee Foster Adoptive Care Association. She is the Walk Me Home Program Coordinator for the National Foster Parent Association. She has worked with children for 30 years. Because of these experiences, she began writing books for children. The first book was a foster care children's book called *Two Ways Home: A Foster Care Journey.* She also has a Facebook blog called Tips from the FLIP Side. FLIP stands for Fully Loving & Inspiring People. It is a blog filled with positivity and helpful information such as recipes, book/movie recommendations, and organizational tips.

About the Illustrator

Rebekah Wood is a Fine Arts student at Winthrop University in Rock Hill, South Carolina. This is her second collaboration with Marion Rhines as she illustrated *Two Ways Home: A Foster Care Journey.* Rebekah continues to advocate for invisible disabilities and loves to share her own story of living with a disability that is not visible. She recently had a neurostimulator implant that allows her to do more than she ever thought she could dream. Rebekah gives these new feelings light in her paintings, prints, and sculptures and will continue to explore new thoughts in future artwork.

Printed in the United States
By Bookmasters